McDUFF STORIES

This book belongs to:
_____

For Dad
with love and admiration
—S.J.

Text copyright © 2002 by Rosemary Wells
Illustrations copyright © 2002 by Susan Jeffers
All rights reserved. No part of this book may be
reproduced or transmitted in any form or by any means,
electronic or mechanical, including photocopying, recording,
or by any information storage and retrieval system,
without written permission from the publisher.
For information address Hyperion Books for Children,
114 Fifth Avenue, New York, New York 10011-5690.
Printed in Hong Kong

First paper-over-boards edition, 2005
1 3 5 7 9 10 8 6 4 2

This book is set in Cochin.
Reinforced binding

ISBN 0-7868-5675-0
Library of Congress Cataloging-in-Publication Data on file.

Visit www.hyperionbooksforchildren.com

SAVES THE DAY

ROSEMARY WELLS • SUSAN JEFFERS

HYPERION BOOKS FOR CHILDREN
NEW YORK

It was the Fourth of July. Lucy and Fred took McDuff and the baby for a picnic at Lake Ocarina.

McDuff rode in the backseat next to the baby, which he did not like, but *with* the fried chicken, which he did like.

McDuff switched to the front seat, where he could see everything, which he liked,

but Lucy's lap was too bumpy and jumpy, which he did not like.

He could not make up his mind where to sit.
So Lucy and Fred stopped the car and gave McDuff a walk
and some cool water.

Lucy took over the driving.
"You can't sit on my lap, McDuff," said Fred.
"You are too hot, heavy, and hairy."

Back went McDuff next to the baby again.
He smelled the fried chicken, warm in the picnic basket.
"Woof!" said McDuff, and the baby woke up.

Lucy stopped the car. Fred gave the baby a bottle.
Lucy gave McDuff a marrowbone so that he wouldn't
bark at the chicken.

"I'll drive," said Fred.
As soon as the baby finished her bottle,
she took the marrowbone away from McDuff.
"Fred, stop the car!" said Lucy. "The baby has the marrowbone!

"I'll drive," said Lucy.
Fred had to sit in the backseat with the baby and the chicken.
"He always gets the front seat in the end," said Fred. McDuff
stretched out in the front seat and fell into a sausage-squirrel dream.

When they arrived at Lake Ocarina, Lucy carried the picnic basket and the baby. Fred carried the beach chairs and the blanket and the Handy Dandy Foldaway Baby Emergency Travel Kit.

"I'll take the baby out in the Float-a-Boat," said Lucy.
"I'll go back and fetch the sun umbrella and the playpen
and the Slug-a-Bug," said Fred.
"You watch our picnic, please, McDuff," said Fred and Lucy.

McDuff knew no one would dare come near the picnic basket with him there. But McDuff didn't hear or smell the silent invaders. They penetrated the picnic basket by the hundreds. In a few short minutes, the picnic was gone.

Lucy and Fred did not know what to do.
"We could eat mulberries," said Lucy.
"I could catch a small fish," said Fred.
McDuff decided to explore other picnics.

He went from blanket to blanket until he found Mr. DiMaggio.
McDuff took a meatball from Mr. DiMaggio's picnic.
"No!" said Mr. DiMaggio.
McDuff started eating more meatballs.

"No! No! No!" said Mr. DiMaggio.
Lucy and Fred heard him.
"Your dog is eating my picnic!" said Mr. DiMaggio.
"We're so sorry!" said Fred and Lucy.

"You see, the ants ate our picnic, and he is hungry!"
"Oh, that's terrible!" said Mr. DiMaggio. "Sit right down and eat.
I have lots extra."

Mr. DiMaggio shared his egg salad, fried chicken, devil's food cake, and lemonade with Lucy, Fred, and the baby.
Lucy gave McDuff a turkey-and-tomato sandwich.

"Without you, we'd have had nothing to eat," said Lucy.
"Without you, I'd have been very lonely," said Mr. DiMaggio.
"But it was McDuff who introduced us and saved the day,"
said Fred.

Dusk fell.

Mr. DiMaggio brought out his concertina.

"Waaaaa!" screamed the baby.

Fred held the baby's ears, but it did no good.

Mr. DiMaggio played "The Star-Spangled Banner."
"Waaaa!" screamed the baby.
Then McDuff began to howl.
And everyone sang along.

It was time to pack up the umbrella and the Float-a-Boat and the
Slug-a-Bug and the Handy Dandy Foldaway Baby Emergency
Travel Kit and say good-bye to Mr. DiMaggio.
"Into the backseat, McDuff!" said Fred.

Suddenly the fireworks began.
Bang! Bang! went the fireworks.
"Waaaa!" screamed the baby.
Fred said, "You'll have to hold your hands over the baby's ears."

"Your hands are bigger and more soundproof," said Lucy.
So Fred stopped the car and got into the backseat with the
baby. Lucy got into the driver's seat, and McDuff came in the
front seat.

"He always gets the front seat," said Fred.
"Yes," said Lucy, "but after all, he saved the day!"